Published by Scholastic Inc.
90 Old Sherman Turnpike, Danbury, Connecticut 06816.

For information regarding permission, write to:
Disney Licensed Publishing
114 Fifth Avenue, New York, New York 10011.

ISBN 0-7172-6813-6

Designed and produced by Bill SMITH STUDIO.

Printed in the U.S.A.
First printing, February 2004

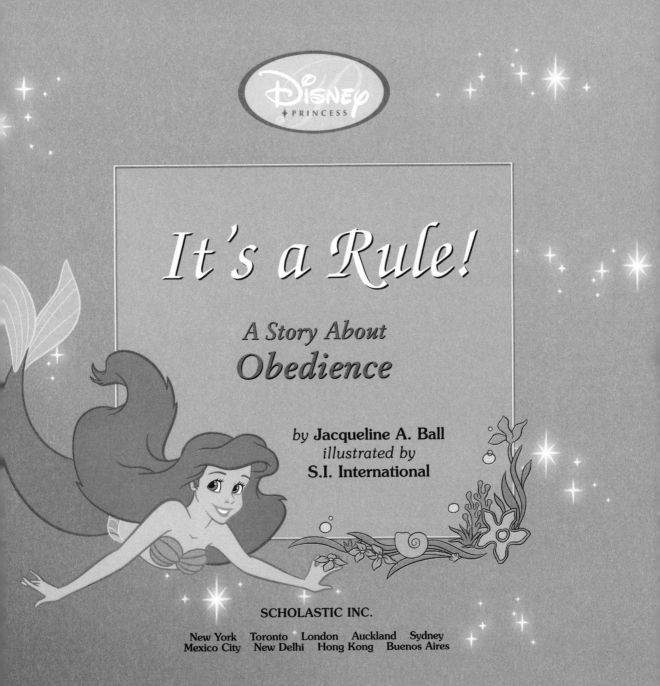

DISNEP
✦ PRINCESS

It's a Rule!

A Story About
Obedience

by **Jacqueline A. Ball**
illustrated by
S.I. International

SCHOLASTIC INC.

New York   Toronto   London   Auckland   Sydney
Mexico City   New Delhi   Hong Kong   Buenos Aires

"Six, seven, eight!" Ariel counted as she played with some pretty stones she had found with Flounder. Ariel was trying to keep them floating at the same time.

"Two more and I'll have a perfect score!" she exclaimed.

"Ariel!" a low, powerful voice called. "Are you still up?"

*T*riton entered the room. "You should be asleep," he told her.

"I'm not tired yet, Daddy," Ariel answered.

Triton removed the glowing eels from their places. "Lights out," he said firmly. "You need your rest, especially because of the sea horse races tomorrow."

*A*riel loved the sea horse races. This year, for the first time, she would be a judge. She couldn't wait!

Triton looked around the room and frowned. "You also need to keep your room clean. I want you to tidy it up tomorrow before you do anything else."

$\mathcal{A}$riel sighed. She wanted to go exploring in the morning. Maybe she would find another sunken ship, full of wonderful human things.

"Don't forget, the races are at noon," Triton added. "Now get some sleep. Good night, Ariel."

"Good night," Ariel said unhappily.

$\mathcal{A}$fter Triton left, Ariel sank onto her pillow. "Do this, don't do that," she muttered. "Why does Daddy have so many rules? And why do I have to obey them all?"

Ariel decided to see what would happen if she disobeyed her father. "I'll stay awake the entire night. That will show him!" she thought. She tried to play with her stone collection again, but she couldn't see well enough in the darkness.

After a while, her eyelids began to droop. Finally, she fell asleep.

$\mathcal{A}$riel woke up late the next morning, feeling tired and cranky. She cleaned her room in a big rush, putting things away anywhere she could find. Then she swam out to find Flounder.

Outside the palace, Sebastian the crab was scurrying around holding some signs.

"Hello, Sebastian. What are those?" Ariel asked.

"*T*riton asked me to put these signs up for the races," Sebastian said importantly.

All Ariel could read on the signs were the words DO NOT. She frowned. More rules to obey!

"Where are you going, Ariel?" Sebastian asked.

"Oh, nowhere special," she said innocently.

Sebastian wagged a warning claw. "Remember, your father told you never to go off alone, Ariel. And he needs to know where you are at all times."

"I know the rules," Ariel replied impatiently. "All 10 million of them!" She turned her tail and swam away.

$\mathcal{A}$riel swam through the water. Where was Flounder? None of the sea creatures had seen him.

"*I*f I wait for Flounder any longer, I won't have time to go exploring before the races," Ariel thought. "I'll just go by myself."

She knew she would be disobeying two rules: going alone, and not telling anyone where she was going. "I don't care," she told herself. "And what difference does it make, anyway?"

But after a while, the water became dark. Ariel was tired from staying up so late. She stopped to rest and brushed up against the side of a big shipwreck.

She swam closer. The sunken boat was full of poles and traps and fishing line. This was the kind of boat humans used to catch fish and sea creatures!

All of a sudden Ariel wanted to go home where it was safe. She started to swim away from the boat, but she was too sleepy. She yawned and closed her eyes for an instant.

When she opened them, she was caught in a huge net! She struggled to get free and became even more tangled.

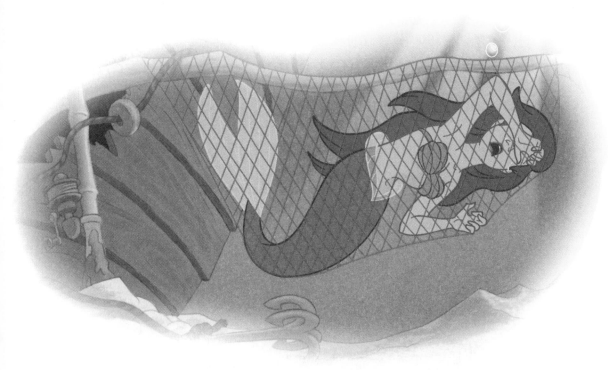

$\mathcal{A}$riel began to cry. Now she would miss the sea horse races. And because no one knew where she was, she might not be found for a long time!

"I wish I had obeyed Daddy's rules," she thought sadly. "Now I know they were for my own good—to keep me safe."

After a very long time, a cheerful swordfish came along. "Princess Ariel," he said. "You seem to be all *tied up*. Lucky I *saw* you! Ha-ha!"

Soon the swordfish had sawed a big hole in the net. Ariel swam through.

Being free gave Ariel a burst of energy. She swooped and swirled through the water. "Thank you so much!" she called as she sped home.

$\mathcal{A}$ few minutes later, Flounder joined her. "Ariel!" he cried. "I've been at the sea horse stables looking for you! The races will start any minute!"

"I was looking for you, too!" she exclaimed. Then she told him what had happened. "Come on, we'd better hurry," she said.

The two friends swam as fast as they could. But when they got to the edge of the racetrack, Ariel stopped short. Sebastian's signs had been set up. Now she could see that they read DO NOT CROSS THIS LINE.

"Hurry, Ariel," Flounder called. "This is the quickest way. If we have to swim all the way around the track, we'll miss the race."

Ariel wanted to be a judge with all her heart.
But the signs were rules, put there by her father to
be obeyed.

DO NOT CROSS
THIS LINE

*W*hat would a princess do?

"No, Flounder," she said. "I disobeyed some of Daddy's rules and got myself in trouble. Now I know those rules were to protect me. There must be a good reason for this rule, too."

*S*uddenly a sea horse sped past. The rider was pulling hard on the reins, trying to stop. "By mistake, we started too soon," the rider called to Ariel. "Good thing you weren't in the way!"

"*I*f we had been crossing, someone could have been hurt!" exclaimed Flounder. "Now I understand what you mean about obeying rules, Ariel."

"I need to show Daddy I'm sorry for disobeying," Ariel said. "And I think I know just how to do it."

Triton saw Ariel and ordered the races to be delayed. When she reached him, he gave her a big hug. "I was so worried about you," he said.

"I disobeyed your rules, Daddy," Ariel said. "But I understand now why you made them, and I want to show you I'm sorry."

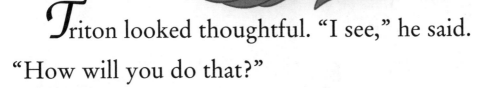

$\mathcal{T}$riton looked thoughtful. "I see," he said. "How will you do that?"

"Because I disobeyed, I shouldn't be a judge this year as my punishment," Ariel said softly. "I'll go to my room until the races are over. Good-bye."

Then Ariel went home.

"*A*re you sad to have missed the races?" Flounder asked.

"Yes, but I learned an important lesson about obeying rules," replied Ariel, yawning. "They keep me safe—and well rested!"

"Since we're here, let's play with your new pretty stones," Flounder suggested.

But Ariel had cleaned her room so fast that now she couldn't find the stones. So she cleaned again—carefully this time. Flounder spotted the sack of stones under the bed.

But it was too late. Ariel was fast asleep.

The End